SUPER Juice
United Sweet!

SUPER Juice
Merged Medley!
All Natural

SUPER Juice
Mixed Marvel!
All Natural

SUPER Juice
Joy!
All Natural

SUPER Juice
Merged Medley!

SUPER Juice
Mixed Marvel!
All Natural

SUPER Juice
Blended Joy!
All Natural

SUPER
Fused Focus!
All Natural

SUPER Juice
Blended Joy!
All Natural

SUPER Juice
Fused Focus!
All Natural

SUPER Juice
United Sweet!
All Natural

SUPER Juice
Merged Medley!

SUPER Juice
Mixed Marvel!
Natural

SUPER Juice
Blended Joy!
Natural

SUPER
Fused Focus
Natural

MIXED ME!

I dedicate this book to Walker, Shane, Olu, Kasey,
Thembi, Amanza, Braker, Noah, and all the crazy-coifed,
buttery-skinned, individual mixties of the world.
Thank y'all for being you and helping me better accept myself.
—T.D.

Thank God for the gift.
Dedicated to my Mother Marie and Father Jackie Vance.
—S.W.E.

A Feiwel and Friends Book
An Imprint of Macmillan

Mixed Me! Text copyright © 2015 by Taye Diggs. Illustrations copyright © 2015 by Shane W. Evans.
All rights reserved. Printed in China by Toppan Leefung, Dongguan City, Guangdong Province.
For information, address Feiwel and Friends, 175 Fifth Avenue, New York, N.Y. 10010.

Library of Congress Cataloging-in-Publication Data Available

ISBN: 978-1-250-04719-9

Book design by Kathleen Breitenfeld and Rich Deas

Feiwel and Friends logo designed by Filomena Tuosto

First Edition: 2015

10 9 8 7 6 5 4 3 2 1

mackids.com

MIXED ME!

by
TAYE DIGGS

Illustrated by
SHANE W. EVANS

FEIWEL AND FRIENDS
NEW YORK

HEY, now!
They call me Mixed-up Mike.
My hair is like WOW!
Super-crazy-fresh-cool, man.
YEAH!

I like to go **FAST!**
No one can stop me
as the wind combs through
my zigzag curly 'do!

"What's happenin', Captain?" my daddy says.
"HI!" I say.
"BYE!" I say.

"Hey, sweet boy, sweet pie, honey boo,"
my mom coos.
She's my one and only, never lonely.

"HI!" I say.
"BYE!" I say.

Sometimes when we're together
people stare at whatever.

"Your mom and dad don't match,"
they say, and scratch their heads.

See, my dad's a deep brown and
my mom's rich cream and honey.
Then people see me, and they look at us funny.

My mom and dad say I'm a blend
of dark and light.
"We mixed you perfectly,
and got you **JUST RIGHT!**"

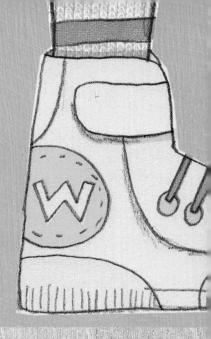

There are so many flavors
to savor and taste!
Why pick only one
color or face?
Why pick one race?

Some kids at school want me to choose
who I cruise with.
I'm down for **FUN** with everyone.

Why pick one race?

I'm a combo plate!
Garden salad, rice and beans—
tasting GREAT!
But wait!

And if they care too much
about my hair too much
that it's not straight enough,
I say, "It's MY HAIR,
don't touch!"

I'm doing my thing, so don't forget it.

If you don't get it, then you don't get it.

UH-HUH, I said it!

I'm a beautiful blend of dark and light,
I was mixed up perfectly,
and I'm JUST RIGHT!

They call me Mixed-up Mike,
but that name should be fixed.
I'm not mixed up,
I just happen to be mixed.

MIXED ME!